Little, Brown and Company

Hachette Book Group
1290 Avenue of the Americas, New York, NY 10104
Visit us at lb-kids.com

Little, Brown and Company is a division of Hachette Book Group, Inc.
The Little, Brown name and logo are trademarks of Hachette Book Group, Inc.

The publisher is not responsible for websites (or their content) that are not owned by the publisher.

First Edition: December 2016
First published in Great Britain in 2016 by Hodder and Stoughton

ISBN 978-0-316-54311-8

10 9 8 7 6 5 4 3 2 1

WKT

PRINTED IN CHINA

The illustrations for this book were created by combining drawing and mark-making on paper with screen printing, and then pieced together digitally.
The text was set in F Caslon Twelve ITC.

LOVE
Matters Most

Written by **Mij Kelly**

Illustrated by **Gerry Turley**

LITTLE, BROWN AND COMPANY
NEW YORK BOSTON

Why is the bear staring into the night,
at a world that is turning shimmering white?

The wind's full of snow. The air's full of frost.

She's looking for something, but what has she lost?

And why would a bear go out in a storm,
leaving a cave that's sheltered and warm?

It must be important. Is she searching for gold...

or ruby-red berries out there in the cold...

or the forest's true magic dancing in light?
Why is she out on such a cold night?

Will she catch salmon leaping from water so clear...

or watch as a snowflake melts to a tear...

or wonder and stop, transfixed in a dream
by faraway stars that glitter and gleam?

No, none of these. There are prints in the snow.
Who could have made them, and where do they go?

She's searching
for someone.
Who could it be?

Look—there's the answer.

Of course, can you see?

Yes, the world's full of treasures and fabulous sights,
but when bear finds her cub, who was lost in the night,

she cuddles him warm and cuddles him close,
and knows, above all...